This book belongs to a
friend of Quirky Claus.
Be warned, those who touch
it may be in for a very
unexpected Christmas!

Your name:

Dedicated to All Those
With a Free Spirit!

Look out for possible future illustrated stories, featuring the adventures of Quirky Claus and his mischievous sidekick Timothy Toucan!

Why not visit www.quirkyclaus.com

First published in Great Britain by White Knights Publishing in 2007

ISBN: 978-0-9554036-0-6

A CIP catalogue record for this title is available from the British Library.

Printed and bound by Reeds Printers, Penrith.

QUIRKY CLAUS!

SEBASTIAN WHITE

White Knights Publishing

WELCOME TO
SOUTH POLE

Not many people know this
but Santa has a cousin,
who happens to live,
not at the North Pole,
but in the deep snow-driven
depths of the South Pole!
HMMM...

His beard is black,
his hair **dazzling** spiky red
and his **amazing** suit,
the **dashing** colour
of indigo.

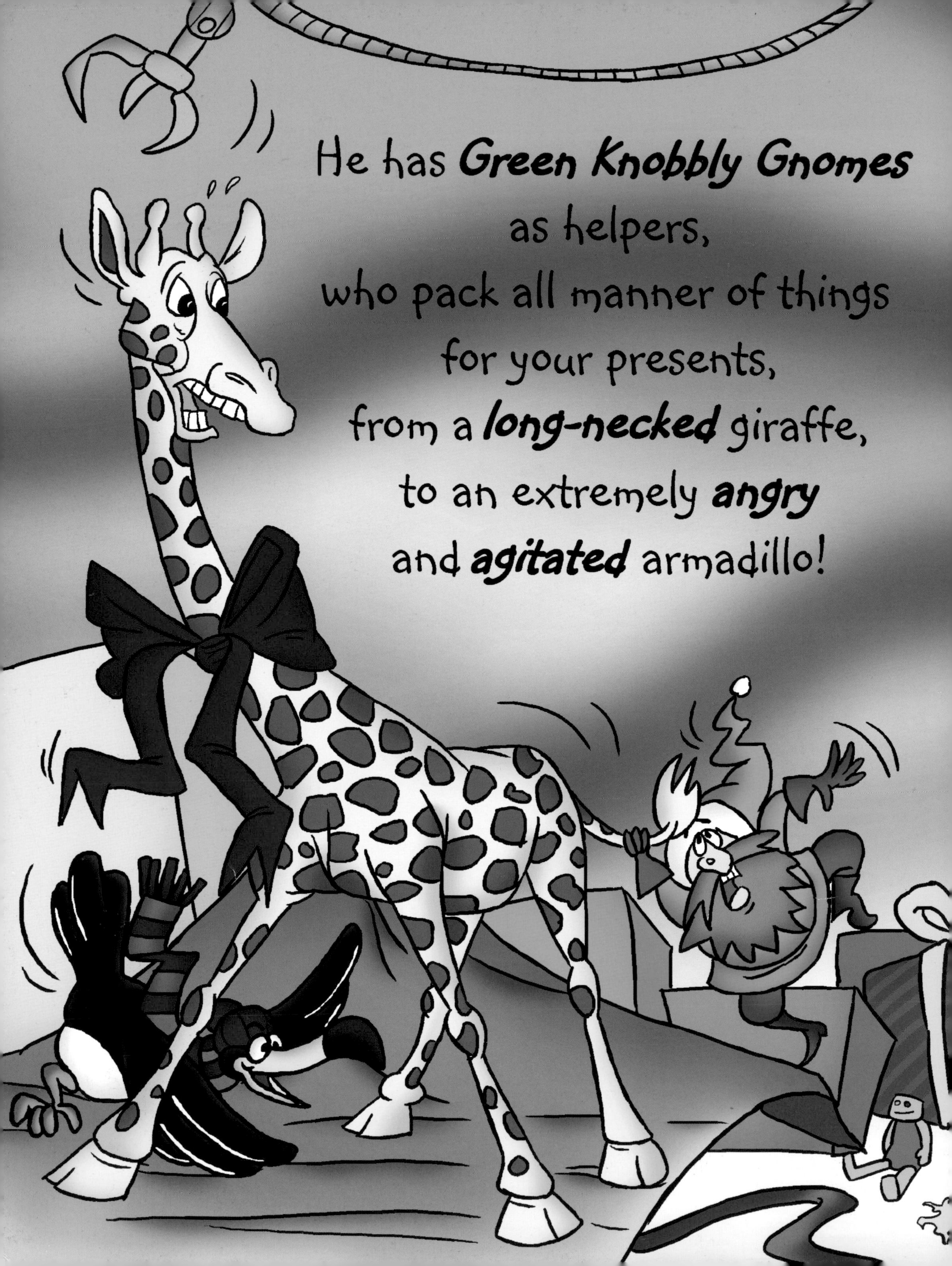
He has **Green Knobbly Gnomes**
as helpers,
who pack all manner of things
for your presents,
from a **long-necked** giraffe,
to an extremely **angry**
and **agitated** armadillo!

His workshop is **old**
and **cranky**
and often **explodes**
in a hail of powder
and **great** big black
puffs of smoke!!!!!!!!!

At Christmas
he delivers the presents
in a ***motorised toboggan***,
as he thinks an ordinary sledge
is ***far*** too slow.

He's tried other means of travelling
but being ***flung*** from a ***bucking***
reindeer is not his idea of having fun!

He crashes regularly
and can be found **stuck** in
the branches of a tree,
caught in a snowdrift or
wrapped around
a rusty old lamppost.

At other times it has not been uncommon
to find him under the sea,
swimming with the sharks.
Sunk in the ***clear***, tropical
waters of Antigua Bay.

And if that isn't bad enough, his foot occasionally **slips** on the pedal and he can find himself **spinning** into the **darkest depths** of outer space!
NASA

Once he is there, he then
has to plan his ***incredible*** escape.
On a passing ***space shuttle***, or
perhaps a very high flying ***jet-plane***.

He's not the best at ***sneaking*** in either. He'll tie ***loose bed sheets*** together and try his hand, attempting a mad ***"Indiana Jones-style"*** swooping swing!

HAPPY
NEW YEAR!!

Only with luck will
he even actually get to where he is going,
but arriving with sacks ***bursting*** full of strange
toys at ***New Year*** is just a little too late!

If all else fails,
he can always count on his ***trusting*** friend
the ***Easter Bunny***
to ***bounce*** around with your presents
and drop them ***right*** in.

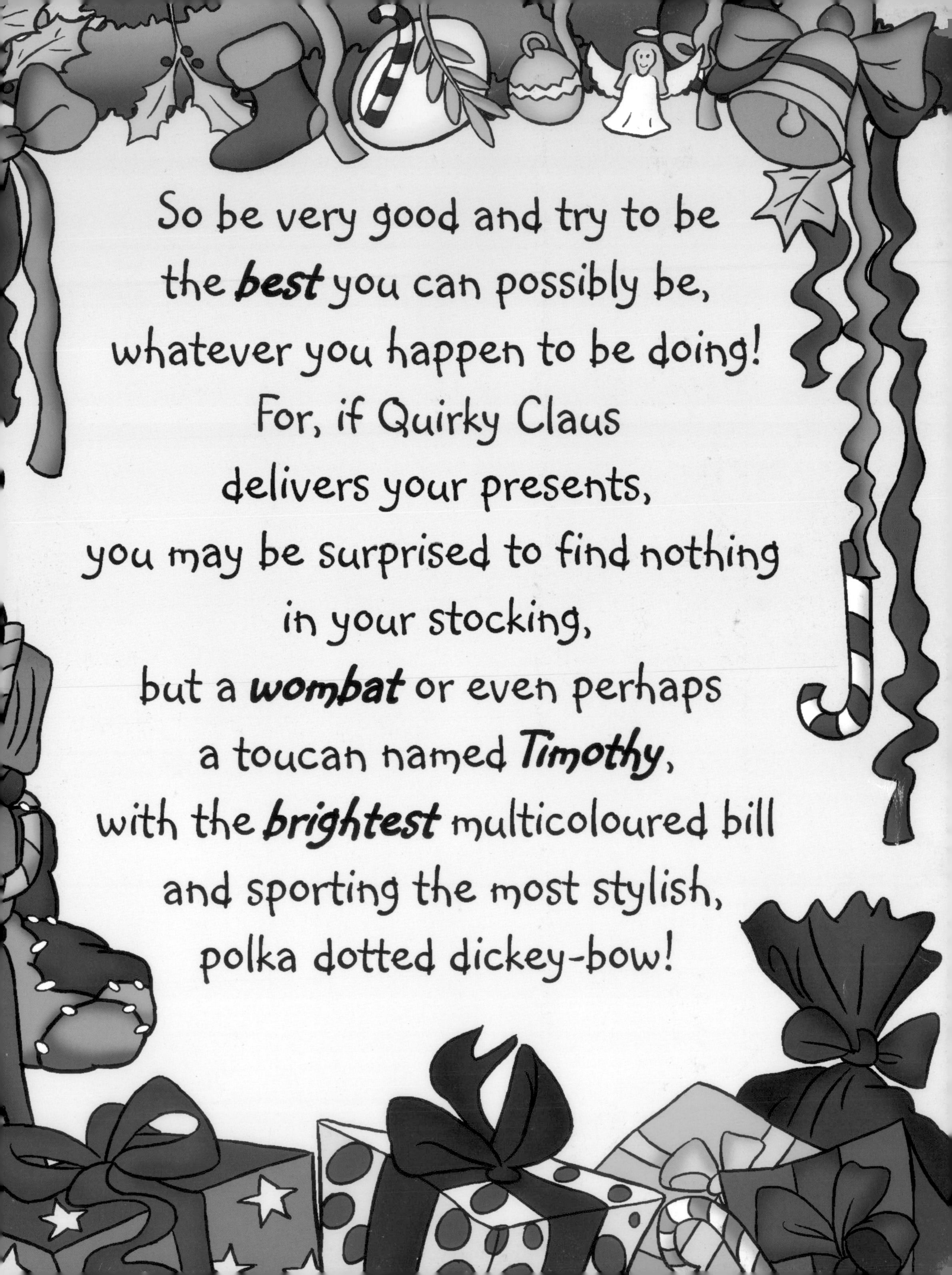

So be very good and try to be
the ***best*** you can possibly be,
whatever you happen to be doing!
For, if Quirky Claus
delivers your presents,
you may be surprised to find nothing
in your stocking,
but a ***wombat*** or even perhaps
a toucan named ***Timothy***,
with the ***brightest*** multicoloured bill
and sporting the most stylish,
polka dotted dickey-bow!

All Aboard For The Toboggan Express

- Days to Christmas countdown
- Hold back time button
- Ejector seat for when Tim's being annoying
- Turbo-boost lever for when Quirky's late for the Meeting of Elves!
- Or the Green Gnobbly Gnomes annual ball!

Questions for Fans of Quirky Claus:

1. Where and at what very *snowy* place does Quirky Claus live?

____ _____ ____

2. Who is Quirky Claus's *best* friend and sidekick?

_______ _______

3. What does Quirky Claus actually fly in, to deliver the naughty children their *unexpected* presents?

__ _________ _________

4. What *animal* with antlers does Quirky Claus get *flung* from, when he tries another means of travelling?

__ _________

5. What *special* fluffy friend of Quirky Claus helps him deliver the presents at Christmas?

____ _______ _______

6. If *you* were helping Quirky Claus, what strange presents would you like to deliver to the naughty children for Christmas?

____

____

____